W9-DDC-905

Ballerinas Don't Wear Glasses

Ballerinas Don't Wear Glasses

written by AINSLIE MANSON

illustrated by DEAN GRIFFITHS

ORCA BOOK PUBLISHERS

SNOW ON THE ROOFTOPS, snow on the trees, snow everywhere! When hc opened his curtains, Ben whooped with joy. The snow on his windowsill looked sticky, packy, perfect for snowballs. It was going to be the best snowball fight ever.

But at breakfast his mother said, "Don't forget, today's the day I'm working late, and you're responsible for Allison."

Ben wished he could trade his sister in for a happy-go-lucky puppy.

After school Ben and his friends picked teams and stacked up their snowballs. He forgot all about Allison.

"One, two, three . . . FIRE!" he shouted. Snowballs flew back and forth across the road.

A blur of color was just visible through the flying snowballs. Someone was standing right in the middle of the war zone. Ben groaned. It was his sister — and he knew Allison. Any minute now she would shriek and shout, or pummel and pout. But she didn't. She just stood there, looking miserable.

Allison had a big, bulky bag over her shoulder. It was her swan costume for tonight's ballet recital. She was so excited, she had been practicing her pirouettes for months. But Allison didn't look excited now — she just looked silly. And she had ruined the best snowball fight ever.

Ben's friends were throwing snowballs at Allison, and Walter's puppies were leaping all over her. Ben threw a snowball too. He was all ready to throw another when he remembered — today he was responsible for Allison.

"Sisters!" he muttered, and he hurled his second snowball at a tree instead.

Ben picked up the white peace flag.

"Cease fire!" he shouted. "We'd better let her pass. She's carrying her costume for the ballet tonight."

"Ben's sister is in the ballet!" one of the boys called out to the others. They all began to laugh and leap about, whirling and twirling and pointing their toes.

"Ally's in the ballet," they chanted. "Ally's in the ballet!"

Ben didn't whirl or twirl or leap. He just stood there, holding the peace flag, wishing he was somewhere else. Allison began to cry and Ben frowned down at her.

"DON'T make it worse by being a cry baby!" he said sternly.

Ben thought again about how much easier it would be to have a dog instead of a sister.

Then he realized why Allison was crying. Walter was still throwing snowballs at her. One hit her in the face. One hit her on the back of the head. Snow trickled down her neck, because her scarf was missing. And as if that wasn't bad enough, Walter's puppies were still pestering her. Ben stopped being cross with his sister and got mad at his friends instead.

"Stop!" he shouted.

But Walter wouldn't stop, and Allison couldn't get up.

One of Ben's snowballs hit Walter in the face. One hit him on the back of the head and snow trickled down *his* neck. Then Walter got mad too.

When it was over, Ben and Walter were sitting in the war zone where Allison had been. Ben had a ripped jacket and no toque. Walter had a bleeding nose. Walter went home, leaving a trail of red dots behind him in the snow.

The best snowball fight in the whole wide world was over, almost before it had begun . . . and Ben's responsibility was nowhere in sight.

Ben found Allison waiting by the back door. She still clung to her big, bulky bag.

"You sure wrecked everything," he said. He unlocked the door and she followed him inside. "Now put that dumb bag down."

"I can't," said Allison.

"Why?"

"Because the strap is all tangled up with my mitts, and my mitts are pinned to my sleeves, and my glasses are all fogged up, and I can't SEE!"

Ben wanted to go and read a good book or watch television or play a computer game. Instead, with a deep sigh, he untangled his sister and hung up her bag.

"Thanks, Ben," she whispered.

As he was leaving the room, he could hear Allison sniffling as she kicked off her boots and tugged off her jacket and snow pants.

He turned around. Allison's hair stuck out, her clothes were wet, and her face was tear stained.

"Okay," he said, "what's the matter, Ally?"

Allison took off her glasses and wiped them on her sleeve. "Everything is the matter," she said. "I'm not a proper ballerina. They said ballerinas don't have pigtails, they don't have missing teeth, and they don't wear glasses!"

"Who said?"

"The other kids in my class said."

Ben remembered that when he was little like Allison, his friends had said he was too fat, too slow and too clumsy to be a soccer player.

"They're probably just jealous," he said.

"And I got the last, worst swan dress in the pile because I was away last week," Allison wailed. "It's ugly. It's disgusting. I have to fix it before tonight, I just have to! But Mom isn't here, and . . . and I can't sew and neither can you and I have a stomach ache."

"I can so sew, Ally!"

Ben laughed at his own silly words. It *was* true. Once he'd sewn a few badges onto his Cub Scout uniform, but that was all the sewing he'd ever done. Why did Mom have to work late? This was a terrible day to be responsible for Allison.

"You can so sew?" Allison asked with a small, hopeful smile.

"Yes, I can so sew," said Ben. "Put the dress on, Ally. It won't be the last, worst swan dress for long!"

Allison stood on a stool in front of her mother's dressing table. She held out the limp, sagging skirt of the last, worst swan dress. "I look like an ugly duckling instead of a beautiful swan!" she said, and her bottom lip began to tremble.

Ben leapt into action. "Monsieur Ben, at your service," he said, circling Allison and rubbing his chin thoughtfully. "Mademoiselle, it will be belle in no time . . . très, très belle!"

He grabbed his mother's lipstick off the dressing table, marked a spot near Allison's knees and reached for the scissors.

"Mademoiselle? I cut here, yes?"

Allison nodded and turned slowly as he cut. Ben was almost beginning to enjoy himself. He was glad, though, that his friends couldn't see him. He felt like the fairy godmother in Cinderella.

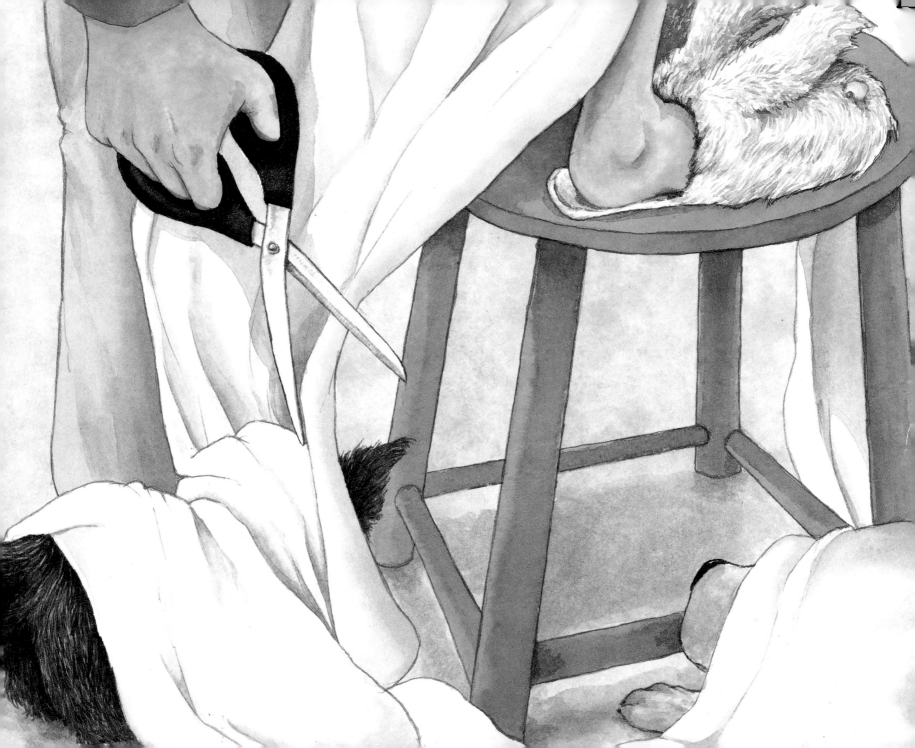

"Thanks," said Allison when he'd finished. But as she hopped down from the stool, she had a good look at the top part of the dress.

"Ben, it droops. They said I'm too skinny and they're right!"

"Ballerinas are supposed to be skinny," said Ben. "It's just that this dress once belonged to an elephant. No wonder it was down at the bottom of the pile." Then he waved his right arm with a flourish. "Pins!" he shouted.

Allison rummaged in her mother's sewing basket and found the pins.

Ben pinned and then he sewed. When he was finished, strange flaps of material grew from Allison's back.

"What are those things?" Allison asked.

Ben thought fast. "Wings," he said.

Allison turned slowly in front of the mirror, examining her wings from every angle.

"You're supposed to be a swan, right? And swans have wings, right?"

Allison nodded. "And I like wings," she said. "Swans can fly and so can I!"

"Right!" said Ben.

Ben made their favorite dinner — peanut butter sandwiches — and then it was time to go. He had a hockey practice at the same time as the ballet recital. He stood ready at the door as Allison struggled into her jacket. She pulled it on backwards.

"*What* are you doing, Ally?" he asked.

"I have to wear it open at the back," she explained, "to protect my wings."

"You can't," he said, zipping it up. "It's just too cold out there."

It *was* cold, and it was dark. The snow squeaked under their boots. Ben struggled along with his hockey bag, his stick, his skates . . . and his pokey sister. He wished she'd hurry.

Finally the school was in sight. Ben was just beginning to think his troubles were over when Allison grabbed him.

"I don't want to dance in front of all those people, Ben. My stomach hurts again."

"You've just got butterflies," Ben said, tugging her along. "Everyone gets butterflies before they go onstage. Remember what you said . . . 'Swans can fly and so can I'?"

"Swans can fly and so can I," Allison repeated in a wobbly, wee voice.

"And anyway," said Ben, "you're way luckier than the rest of those ballerinas."

"ME? Why?"

"Because you can just take off your glasses and then you can't *see* the audience!"

Allison grinned. "So that's why ballerinas don't wear glasses!"

The school lights shone out across the snow. Ballerinas were arriving with their families.

"So long, Ally," said Ben, reaching down and giving one of her pigtails a friendly tug.

"Ben!" she shrieked.

"That did *not* hurt!" said Ben.

"No . . . no, it didn't. But . . . but it made me remember the other thing that ballerinas DON'T!" Allison hopped up and down like a kangaroo. "They DON'T have pigtails, Ben! Mom was supposed to put my hair up!"

Ben frowned. "Your teacher will help you."

"Nooooo," Allison wailed, "she's too busy! Our mothers were supposed to fix our hair."

Ben looked over at the rink. None of his friends had arrived yet.

"Then I'll help you," Ben said, "if you stop crying."

He sat down on the school steps and removed the lace from one of his skates.

"Sit," he ordered, and Allison sat down beside him.

Ben bunched her pigtails together and wound the lace round and round until the hair was secure. "There," he said, "your pigtails are up."

Allison dried her tears with a snowy mitt
and gave him a broad, toothless grin.
"Thanks," she said.

"It was nothing," said Ben.

When Allison disappeared through the
door, Ben looked at the skate in his hand and
laughed. How was he going to skate with only
one lace? He decided to skip hockey practice
and watch Allison being a swan instead.

Ben got two seats, front row center. His mother arrived just as the curtain was going up.

"Did you have any problems with Allison?" she asked.

"Not really," Ben replied, his eyes on the rising curtain.

"Where are her glasses?" Mom whispered, when Allison came onstage.

"Ballerinas don't wear glasses," Ben whispered back.

"And why is she the only one with wings?"

Ben shrugged. "She's the only real swan."

Ben held his breath — Allison was doing her solo. Her pigtails stayed put and her pirouettes were perfect. Allison really *was* a swan. She *did* fly.

When the ballet was over, Allison came forward to the front of the stage and curtsied gracefully. She had her glasses back on and she smiled at the audience. Ben whistled and waved and clapped extra hard.

Maybe, just maybe, he wouldn't trade her in for a happy-go-lucky puppy after all.

Text copyright © 2000 Ainslie Manson
Illustration copyright © 2000 Dean Griffiths

Canadian Cataloguing in Publication Data
Manson, Ainslie.
Ballerinas don't wear glasses

ISBN 1-55143-176-9 (pbk)

I. Griffiths, Dean, 1967 – II. Title.
PS8576.A567B34 2000 jC813'.54 C99-911331-3
PZ7.M31812Ba 2000

Library of Congress Catalog Card Number: 99-069235

Orca Book Publishers gratefully acknowledges the support of
our publishing programs provided by the following agencies:
the Department of Canadian Heritage,
The Canada Council for the Arts, and the British
Columbia Arts Council.

Design by Christine Toller
Printed and bound in Korea

IN CANADA:
Orca Book Publishers
PO Box 5626, Station B
Victoria, BC Canada
V8R 6S4

IN THE UNITED STATES:
Orca Book Publishers
PO Box 468
Custer, WA USA
98240-0468

02 01 00   5 4 3 2

E   Easy
Mans

Manson, Ainslie
Ballerinas don't· wear glasses

GAYLORD M